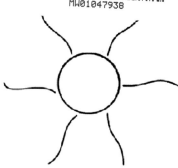

Chickwick

The

Easter

Gift

Based on a true story

by Alice Curtis

Interactive story/coloring book

Scripture reference from the King James Version

To Mom

Thanks for always believing.

One Easter Sunday Morning Mom brought a surprise

And when my brother and I looked we could hardly believe our eyes.

In a little cardboard box filled with colored straw

It was a baby chick of yellow we saw.

We knew that whenever Easter season came around

That marshmallow candies and chocolate bunnies abound.

But we didn't ever think we'd be given such a gift on this day

This wonderful, unusual pet. "No way!"

Yet Easter is much more than chocolate and jelly beans

But for a long time us kids never paid attention to what it really means.

It proclaims the gift of forgiveness, salvation and new life through God's Son

But we just thought spring flowers, new clothes, a little church and some fun.

But this Resurrection Sunday was indeed a day of birth

For we had a baby chick all new to this earth.

We petted and loved it and gave it a name;

We called it "Chickwick" and our life would never be the same!

While Chickwick was young he was content in his box

But soon that tiny chick started to grow and needed a lot.

More than a daily romp in the grass was needed for to our great surprise

He became a white-feathered,

red-combed rooster right before our eyes!

He started to try out his wings, peck the box and leap

Up on the side of the box so all around he could peep.

He'd open his eyes before the dawn and if you weren't awake

Well, Old Chickwick would wake you up, make no mistake!

He would jump up onto the edge of his box

Then he'd take in a breath and he'd look at the clock.

And when the big hand was on the 12 and the little on the 6

He'd let out a "cock-a-doodle-doo" without a hitch.

Now we loved that dear rooster, the Easter gift, that Mom gave

But I tell you we sure tried hard to make him behave.

You see Chickwick was bold and he greeted each day

With a bellow that roosters for centuries have made!

Now one day dear Chickwick became too much to bear

And to keep him confined, in a box, seemed a little unfair.

So, we packed up his belongings and jumped in the car

To take him to the "country" where other roosters are.

When we let dear old Chickwick out in the yard

He looked around unfamiliar, at first, but it wouldn't be hard

For him to adjust to wide-open spaces and blue sky

And a little while later he left without a goodbye.

Our house was lonely and empty after Chickwick was gone

But the 6AM quiet gave us strength to carry on.

While down in the "country" Chickwick was ruling the land

He was the king of the barnyard and it wasn't hard to understand.

'Cause he always had something that made him that way

He was confident and bold and eagerly welcomed each day.

So down in the country with more land to spare

Chickwick became the ruler of the roost and lived without a care.

That Chickwick of ours was not just a part of the crowd

So, on the door of the house he'd peck and peck loud.

For he wanted to have his food straight from the source

And he was used to being hand fed and that had to continue of course.

Chickwick, each day, would go to the door

And there he would peck and they'd give him some more.

Yes, after a while it was just as it would be

That the king of the roost was fed as he should be!

Oh, Chickwick was a chicken but it seems to me

That he must have known the Resurrection miracle that makes us all free.

For he was not just an ordinary rooster in a childhood rhyme

He was Chickwick, bold and strong, born at Easter time!

Thanks be unto God for his unspeakable gift.

2 Corinthians 9:15

The End

Made in the USA
Middletown, DE
19 April 2025

74512986R00022